Princess Stories

✳ ✳

Once upon a time in a village in
Northamptonshire, there lived a woman
called Anna Wilson. She was not a
princess. She didn't live in a castle, or even
a palace. She was married to David, who
was handsome (but not a prince). She had
a daughter called Lucy and a son called
Thomas and two black cats called Ink and
Jet. She wanted to get a dog and call it
Printer. And then she would live happily
ever after.

✳

✳

Look out for

Fairy Stories

Princess Stories

Chosen by **Anna Wilson**

Illustrated by Lara Jones

MACMILLAN CHILDREN'S BOOKS

For Gaby Morgan and Rachel Denwood –
my fairy godmothers

First published 2005 by Macmillan Children's Books
A division of Macmillan Publishers Limited
20 New Wharf Road, London N1 9RR
Basingstoke and Oxford
www.panmacmillan.com

Associated companies throughout the world

ISBN 0 330 43797 6

1 3 5 7 9 8 6 4 2

A CIP catalogue record for this book is available from
the British Library.

Typeset by Nigel Hazle
Printed and bound in Great Britain by Mackays of Chatham plc, Kent

Contents

The Sixteenth Princess
by Jeremy Strong   1

The Frog Princess
by Alan Durant   27

The Twelve Dancing Princesses
by Saviour Pirotta   38

The Princess and the Pea
by Sally Gardner   58

A Wreath of Wild Roses
by Barbara Sleigh   69

The Princess's New Nose
by Anna Wilson   101

Cinderella Rap
by Tony Mitton   131

The Reluctant Dragon and
the Wilful Princess
by William Raeper   147

The Little Mermaid
by Anna Wilson   211

Princess Dragonbreath
by Fiona Dunbar   238

The Sixteenth Princess

Jeremy Strong

When Belinda was born her father, King Stormbelly, took one look at her and said, 'Ugh!' Belinda's mother smiled mildly and observed that princesses never looked their best at two o'clock in the morning, especially when they were only one hour old. As for Belinda, she let out such an almighty wail that the king stuffed his fingers in his ears and fled back to bed.

As time went by Belinda lost her creased-up wrinkles and began to look altogether more attractive, though never beautiful. King Stormbelly decided that something had gone wrong with the child. He had sixteen children. They were all girls, they were all princesses and they were all astonishingly beautiful and talented . . . all except for

Belinda, who was quite ordinary. But she did have eyes of a most serene blue. The king never seemed to notice Belinda's eyes.

'I don't know what we're going to do about her,' grumbled King Stormbelly, as Belinda grew up and showed no signs of becoming a ravishing beauty. 'All the

other princesses will find husbands easily, but nobody will be foolish enough to marry her. She's not even particularly clever.'

The queen didn't say anything because she knew that if she started to argue, Stormbelly would fly into one of his silly tempers, start kicking the guards and hurt his feet on their heavy armour. Then he'd take to his bed and stay there for a week, pretending all his toes were broken and it was all the queen's fault.

So the queen didn't say anything,

4

but she thought a great deal. She was very fond of all her daughters and especially pleased that fifteen of them were astonishingly beautiful. But she was even more pleased that Belinda was different. What's more, she knew that Belinda was a lot cleverer than her father and it was only because Belinda always beat her father playing Snap that the king was so grumpy about her.

All the same, the king was quite right when he said that the fifteen beautiful princesses would easily find husbands, whereas Belinda would have to do a bit of work if she ever wanted to marry. The queen thought about all these things and then decided what ought to be done.

First of all she went to Belinda very quietly and whispered in her ear, 'Belinda dear, the next time you play Snap with your father please make sure that you lose.'

'Oh, Mum!' Belinda didn't like losing at anything. 'Do I have to?'

The queen nodded and Belinda

sighed, but the next time she played
a game with her father she lost.

'Snap!' cried Stormbelly
triumphantly. 'Ha ha! You've got
to have sharp eyes to beat me,
Belinda.'

'Yes, Dad. I can see that,' the

youngest princess murmured shamefacedly.

Off went the king, singing and dancing down the palace corridors, swinging round on the arms of the astonished guards and making them dance with him, until at last he reached the queen.

'You seem very cheerful, dear,' she mused.

'Ha ha! Do you know I've just won a game of Snap. Old sharp eyes, that's me!' He held his big belly and laughed.

The queen smiled too. 'Oh, I am pleased.'

'Ah,' said the king, sitting down with a soft thud. 'She's not such a bad girl, Belinda.'

'I've been thinking that too, dear. Do you know, I thought it might be a good idea to get her a tutor.' The queen folded her neat little hands in her lap and smiled at the king.

'A tutor?' queried the king. 'Do you mean a teacher?'

'Yes, if you like. A teacher.'

9

'Whatever for?' demanded
Stormbelly gruffly.

'Well, to teach her, of course.'

'Yes, yes. I know that. But what's
the point?'

'I know that you have been very
worried about Belinda and what
will happen to her when she's
older. I thought that if she was
taught, then she would stand a
better chance later on of finding a
husband.'

King Stormbelly frowned and
twisted his whiskers and scratched

10

his head and snorted a bit. They were all signs that he hadn't got the foggiest idea what he was supposed be thinking about.

'I don't see how having a teacher will help,' he ventured.

'All the other princesses are beautiful and accomplished and will easily find husbands,' explained the queen. 'But Belinda will have to find hers with her brain, if she wants one.'

'Of course she wants one! Whoever heard of a princess who

11

didn't want a husband?' snapped Stormbelly.

'Anyway,' continued the queen, choosing to ignore the king's last remark, 'we ought to do something about Belinda's brain to help her. Don't you think?'

Stormbelly didn't think very much, but it seemed to make sense. And he didn't want Belinda to find things difficult later on. She was a good girl – he'd just beaten her at Snap and that proved it. He gave a small grunt.

12

'All right. Good idea. Make the arrangements and get her a teacher.'

So it was that Hiro Ono came to the palace. Hundreds of people from everywhere applied for the post of teacher to the Princess Belinda (it was highly paid), and the queen had private conversations with them all. For days there was a queue over a mile long, stretching out of the palace gates and right down into the town. The interviews lasted for over a week and at the end of it

13

the queen announced that Hiro
Ono, master tutor from Japan,
would be Belinda's new teacher.

Belinda wasn't very happy about
it. She didn't like the look of Hiro
Ono, with his strange silk robe

that had red and

green dragons

swirling around on

it, and his thin eyes

and bent back. He

had a wispy

beard too,

like an old

spider's web caught on his chin. But Hiro Ono smiled at her and bowed, and they went away together to begin classes.

The years passed and Stormbelly hardly saw Belinda. In fact, he almost forgot about her altogether. The queen didn't. She visited Belinda and Hiro Ono every day to see how they were getting on, and day by day Belinda became more and more fond of Hiro Ono because he taught her such fascinating things.

15

The other fifteen daughters got married, one by one, each to a rich and handsome prince, and went off to start new lives in their husbands' castles. Stormbelly's castle began to seem quite empty and all at once he realized that somewhere in the vast palace he had a sixteenth daughter who wasn't at all beautiful, but it was time she got married. He sent for Belinda.

She and her mother arrived with Hiro Ono trailing softly behind them, a little more bent with age and his beard a little longer.

Belinda had changed too. She was slim and much taller, and her blue eyes were as clear as the blue of a winter sky. Her black hair was cut short, and she regarded her father with a little smile.

'Well,' declared the king, 'how you've grown!' Belinda nodded. 'I hear you've been taught a great deal over the last seven years.'

'Yes, Father,' said Belinda gently.

'Hmmm. Very useful thing, knowledge. So — you've learned lots and lots. Well now, tell me, um, what are three sixes?'

Belinda shrugged. 'I don't know.'

'You don't know!' King Stormbelly was cross. He had hoped she would be able to tell him because he didn't know the answer himself. Belinda turned to Hiro Ono.

'Do you know what three sixes are?' she asked.

'I know what they aren't,' he said slowly. 'They aren't a husband. They are not the clouds enclosing the mighty head of a mountain—'

'What is he going on about?' burst out the king. 'Is he mad?'

The queen gently touched her husband on the arm. 'I think it is Hiro Ono's way of telling you that it doesn't matter what three sixes are. They are not important.'

'Not important! But I've always wanted to know what three sixes are! All right then, let's see how much this nitwit has taught Belinda. Daughter, tell me, what's the capital city of Rome?'

The queen nudged him. 'Rome *is* a capital city,' she whispered.

'Oh, all right. What's the capital city of Spain?'

Belinda couldn't answer that either, and Stormbelly began to hop from one foot to the other. The queen could see that he was getting ready to kick a few guards and probably Hiro Ono himself.

'Why don't you ask Belinda to show you what she *can* do?' she suggested sweetly.

'Fine, fine. Go ahead. Show us

20

what you can do, though I shall be very surprised if it's anything at all,' cried the king, giving Hiro Ono a very dark look.

Belinda looked slowly about the palace hall. Standing at the foot of the stairs was a large stone statue of a previous king. Belinda walked silently up to it, gazed at it for a few moments then suddenly –

'Aaaa-HA!' She gave a great yell, spun round on one foot and launched her other foot at the centre of the statue. There was a splinter of breaking stone and the statue cracked into two separate halves. Even as the top section toppled to the floor, Belinda raised her right arm and sliced the head off with a single blow of her bare hand.

Stormbelly screamed, 'Stop! That's your great-grandfather!'

Belinda grinned back and began to walk up the stairway, chopping the thick wooden banisters into little pieces as she did so. Bits of wood cascaded down at the king's feet and came tumbling down the steps.

'Guards!' yelled the king. 'Stop her before she destroys the whole palace!' Up went the guards in hot pursuit, but no sooner did they reach Belinda than she sent them flying with a few well-aimed kicks and blows from her hands. Then she came down to the bottom of the stairs, bowed to her father, bowed to Hiro Ono and her mother and sat down, brushing the dust from her clothes.

Stormbelly sat down too. He collapsed in an armchair. 'Just what have you been teaching my daughter?' he managed to whisper at length.

'The ancient Japanese art of karate,' said Hiro Ono with a little bow.

Stormbelly shook his head. 'I can't believe it. Did she really do that with her bare hands and feet?'

'Of course,' said Hiro Ono. 'But karate is about strength of mind, not of hands and feet. Your wife, who is very wise, explained your daughter's problem to me. Belinda is a very good pupil. She has a very quick brain. Now she can go into the world and you needn't worry.'

'Needn't worry!' cried the king. 'I shall be terrified with her on the loose, smashing up statues and demolishing staircases all over the place.'

Hiro began to explain that it wouldn't be like that at all, but the queen signalled that the king didn't understand and it wasn't worth explaining. She persuaded the king to have an afternoon sleep while they cleared up the hall.

'Well, you've certainly impressed your father, Belinda,' laughed the queen when everything was sorted out. 'Let's hope you can impress a prince!'

The Frog Princess

Alan Durant

There was once a princess who was very beautiful – as fairy-tale princesses usually are. She had hair as blonde and wavy as pine wood shavings and her skin was as fine and delicate as bone china. Her eyes were bluer than sapphires. Her nose — well, you get the point. She was beautiful.

Not only was this princess beautiful, but she was incredibly vain. Her room was full of photographs of herself in amazing outfits and she spent hours every day admiring her face in the mirror. She couldn't walk past a window without staring at her reflection. Worse still, though, she was very unkind and had a nasty habit of laughing at anyone less fortunate than herself.

One day this princess happened to
be walking by a pond, gazing at
herself in the water, when she spied
an old and ugly woman. And when
I say ugly, I mean ugly. Her whole

face was covered in hairy warts and moles, her teeth were black and broken and she had an enormous beard. As soon as the princess saw the old woman, she started to laugh. She laughed and laughed.

'What is so funny, my dear?' grunted the old lady (no, her voice wasn't beautiful either).

'You, you ugly old crone!' shrieked the princess and she laughed even more, which wasn't at all kind – or at all clever as it turned out, because the old lady was in fact a witch.

'Well, the joke's on you,' hissed the witch and, with a flash of her wand, she turned the princess into a frog. Bam! Just like that. Then off she skipped, cackling like a cauldron.

★

At first, the princess was very upset about the way things had turned out – well, you would be, wouldn't you? Imagine looking into the water and seeing not the beautiful face of a princess but a green and spotty one with big bulgy eyes. Still, after a while, she started to get used to being a frog. And actually, as frogs go, she was quite a stunner, and had lots of male frogs hopping about after her, asking to share her lily pad.

★

Now, one hot day a prince was riding by and stopped at the pond for a paddle. He was a handsome chap, as fairy-tale princes usually are. His hair was as dark as chocolate and his eyes as green as emeralds. His lips were soft and peachy. Imagine his surprise when a frog started talking to him and telling him, in a little croaky voice, that she was really a beautiful princess who had been cursed by a wicked witch.

'How beautiful were you?' the prince asked.

'Very,' said the Frog Princess. And she told him all the stuff about her hair and skin and eyes. This interested the prince very much because he was looking for a beautiful princess just like that for himself and, as yet, he hadn't found one.

'How can I lift the curse?' he asked.

'You have to kiss me,' said the Frog Princess quickly. She rather fancied a kiss from this handsome prince with his soft, peachy lips. Well, it would be a lot nicer than being snogged by a frog!

The prince thought. He thought long, and he thought hard. He wasn't the brightest prince in the world and it made his head spin. He didn't really fancy kissing a frog very much. I mean she wasn't bad-looking for a frog, but she *was* still a frog. And a little on the slimy side. But, if it meant having his very own beautiful princess, well, that had to be worth it.

'You're on,' he said at last. So the prince picked up the Frog Princess, puckered his lips and gave her a kiss, smack on the cheek, and . . .

Bam!

He turned into a frog!

So now the Frog Princess had a Frog Prince to keep her company and they set up home together on the largest, loveliest lily pad in the pond. All the other frogs agreed they made a perfect couple. As it turned out, the prince and princess were better frogs than they had been people and, as in all the best froggy fairy tales, they lived hoppily ever after.

The Twelve Dancing Princesses

Saviour Pirotta

There was once a king who had
twelve beautiful daughters. He was
very proud of them and kept a close
eye on them all day long. At

bedtime he locked them all in one vast bedroom with twelve beds, to make sure they were safe. In the morning he unlocked their door himself, with a golden key he kept on a chain around his neck.

One morning, when the king unlocked the bedroom door, he saw that the princesses' satin shoes had been danced to pieces. No one knew how the princesses had managed to escape from their room, nor who they had danced with. And they weren't saying, no matter

39

how much their father pleaded with them or scolded them.

The same thing happened the next night and the night after that. The mystery bothered the king and, when it seemed that the princesses would not stop sneaking out of the palace, he decided to solve it once and for all.

He sent out a proclamation, inviting all the young men of the land to discover the princesses' secret. Anyone who did, could choose one of the king's daughters to marry and would inherit the kingdom. But anyone who tried and failed three nights in a row would lose his head on the executioner's block.

Many a dashing young prince accepted the challenge. In turn, each was given a sumptuous supper and at bedtime was shown to a chamber adjoining the princesses' bedroom. The door between the two rooms was kept open, so the prince could observe the king's daughters.

But, in turn, each prince fell asleep at his task and in the morning, the princesses' shoes were found tattered and torn. Many princes lost their lives, and the princesses' secret remained just that: a secret.

Now it so happened that a poor soldier found himself on the outskirts of the city where the king lived. He had been wounded in battle and discharged with a medal, but he had no idea where he was to settle or how he was going to earn a living. By chance he met a kind old woman who, seeing the pain and weariness in his face, said, 'Where are you going, my son?'

And he replied jokingly, 'I have no idea, but I might try and discover where the king's daughters dance at night; then I could become king.'

'In that case,' said the woman, who was really a kind witch, 'do not drink the wine that the princesses offer you, because it will have a sleeping potion in it. Just pretend to be fast asleep and, when the princesses go out, follow them closely.' She handed the soldier a cloak. 'Put this on your shoulders,' she whispered, 'and it will make you invisible; that way you can observe the girls without being seen yourself.'

The soldier thanked the old woman and hurried to the palace. Even though he looked poor, he was as well received as the princes had been. He was given a delicious supper and shown to the room adjoining the princesses' chamber.

44

As he was about to get into bed, the eldest offered him a goblet of wine. The soldier pretended to drink it but, when the girl wasn't looking, he emptied the goblet into the chamber pot under the bed. Then he lay down, yawned and began to snore loudly.

'The fool is asleep already,' said the eldest princess. 'The journey to the palace must have tired him out.'

'Poor wretch,' said another, 'he is sure to lose his head in three days' time.'

Then the twelve princesses put on silk party dresses, jewelled crowns and satin dancing shoes. Just before leaving, they took one last look at the soldier to make sure he was still asleep.

'Are you certain he will not wake up before the

morning?' asked the youngest
princess. 'I have an awful feeling
that something dreadful is about to
happen.'

'You are
always in
dread of
one thing or
another,'
mocked the eldest.
'There is nothing to
fear.' Then she
knocked on one of
the beds and it

sank into the floor, revealing a secret staircase. The princesses descended through the opening, one after another.

The soldier, who had secretly been watching everything from his bed, put on his magic cloak and quickly followed them. It was dark in the passage and, halfway down the stairs, he trod on the youngest princess's gown.

'We're being followed,' cried the princess. 'Someone has just tugged on my gown.'

'Don't be foolish,' said the eldest sister. 'You must have caught your dress on a nail.'

At the bottom of the stairs was a garden full of silvery trees, which shone brightly and filled the place with light. The soldier, unable to help himself, reached out and snapped off a twig.

'Did none of you hear that noise?' said the youngest princess. 'I am sure we are not alone.'

'It is only our princes who wait for us,' scolded the eldest princess.

49

She led
the way into a
second garden,
where the trees were
made of gold, and
then on to a
third, where
the trees
were laden with diamonds. In each
garden, the soldier broke off a twig
and the youngest princess gasped at
the sound, but she did not say

anything else to her sisters for fear of being ridiculed.

At last the princesses reached the shores of the lake. The soldier, coming up behind them, saw twelve handsome princes, each one sitting in a boat with a golden lion's head on the prow. Every princess got into a boat, and the soldier – fearing he might be left behind – hopped in with the youngest.

'The boat seems very heavy tonight,' said her prince as he rowed.

'It must be the summer heat,' said the youngest princess. 'I feel a bit tired and listless too.'

Soon all the twelve boats were moored outside a palace on the other side of the lake. Each prince took his princess by the hand and led her up a flight of marble steps into a beautiful ballroom. There, the happy couples danced to the sound of music, the princesses whirling gaily around in their satin shoes. The soldier danced too, and every time he brushed past the

youngest princess she would stifle a
gasp and say, 'I can feel a presence
in this room; I am sure of it.'

By three o'clock, the princesses' shoes were worn to shreds. It was time for them to leave, and their princes rowed them back across the lake. This time the soldier sat next to the eldest princess, and she did not notice his presence, because she was so tired and sleepy.

When they got to the secret passage, the soldier hurried on ahead and jumped back into bed. The princesses, peeping into his room, heard him snoring and assumed that he had been asleep all

54

the time they were gone.

The next night, the soldier followed the princesses again. Everything happened as before and the princesses danced until their shoes were worn to pieces. On the third night, the soldier stole a wine goblet from the food table in the ballroom, which he hid under his cloak.

At last it was time for the soldier to be summoned before the king. 'Have you solved the mystery yet?' asked the king. 'Where do my

55

daughters go at night? And who do they dance with?'

'I have solved the mystery, Your Majesty,' replied the soldier. 'Your daughters escape through a secret tunnel to a palace on the shores of an underground lake. There they dance with twelve handsome princes who row their boats across the water to fetch them.'

He showed the king the silver, gold and diamond twigs and gave him the wine goblet. The king called the princesses at once and, seeing the evidence in the soldier's hands, they confessed all.

So the king asked the soldier to choose one of the princesses as his bride, and he took the eldest, because she had a mischievous smile and was the closest to him in age. The wedding was held that very same day, with much feasting, singing, and, needless to say, dancing. Everyone at the party danced until their shoes had fallen to pieces.

The Princess and the Pea

Sally Gardner

Once upon a time
there lived a prince
who wished very much to
marry a real princess.
His search for a bride
took him around the
world and back

again, which is a very long way indeed.

He met lots of girls who called

themselves princesses: pretty ones,
plain ones, vain ones, happy ones,
sad ones and mad ones. But there
was always something not quite
right. It was a problem. How was
he to know if they were real
princesses?

At last he gave up and went
home, feeling very upset. The king
and queen agreed with their son.
There was no point in marrying a
girl who was not a real princess.
What was to be done?

Then, one wild and stormy night,

a princess was being driven home from a party when her car went too fast round a corner, and she was thrown into a ditch. The chauffeur did not see what had happened and drove on, leaving the princess all alone.

'Well, this is a pickle,' said the princess, picking herself up. 'No point staying here. I'd better try and find some shelter.'

She stumbled through the howling gale and pouring rain until she came to a palace.

'There must be someone here who can help me,' the princess said to herself. So she rang the bell and was brought before the king and queen. She looked a terrible mess. Her hair was dripping wet, her dress was torn, her shoes were all muddy and she had lost her crown.

The king and queen were surprised that this girl called herself a princess, but they were kind enough to invite her to stay. She could not very well go out again on a night like this.

After she had had a bath and been given some clean clothes, the princess was brought to the great hall for supper. The prince thought she looked very nice, but what was the point of falling in love when she might not be a real princess at all?

The queen had an idea. 'Too many girls these days,' she said, 'pretend to be princesses. There is only one way of knowing for certain if this is a *real* princess.'

So the queen went into the girl's bedroom and placed one tiny pea under the mattress. Then she ordered twenty more mattresses to be put on top. She was still not sure if there were enough mattresses, so she ordered another twenty to be put on top of them.

When the princess went to bed she needed a ladder to climb to the top of all those mattresses, but because she was a guest she couldn't very well ask why there were so many when just one would have done nicely.

The bed, for all its forty-one

mattresses, was very uncomfortable. The princess was sure the mattresses were filled with rocks instead of feathers.

In the morning the king and

queen asked her how she had slept.

'I couldn't sleep at all, Your Majesty,' said the princess. 'The bed was so lumpy and bumpy that I am bruised black and blue all over.'

The king and queen were delighted. There could be no doubt that this was a real princess, for only a real princess is tender enough to feel one tiny pea through so many mattresses. The prince was keen to marry her. The princess was happy to marry him too, for it is not easy to find a real prince these days. *Real* princes are rare.

You can see that this prince and princess were made for each other. In no time at all they were married, and they lived happily ever after. Now, isn't that a tender-hearted tale?

As for the pea, it was put in a museum, or was it the soup? Do you know? I quite forget.

A Wreath of Wild Roses
A French Folk Tale

Retold by Barbara Sleigh

Once upon a time, there was a woodcutter, who had two daughters. Both had blue eyes and rosy cheeks and golden hair when they were little girls, but as they grew up Maria became bad-tempered and sour as a

green apple, so that her face was covered with crosspatch wrinkles, and because she was too lazy to brush it, her hair looked grey and dusty and hung down like a wet mop. If everyone called her ugly, it was entirely her own fault. But her sister, Mariette, was as pretty as a clean, cheerful, willing face could make her.

One day, when the woodcutter came home from work, he said, 'Bless my buttons if I haven't left my axe behind in the forest. Now I shall have to go all the way back to fetch it, and me with a great blister on my heel!'

'Don't worry, Father,' said Mariette, 'I'll go and fetch it for you.' And she gave him a kiss and set out, while Maria just scowled, and hid herself so that no one should ask her to go too.

Mariette had barely started on her walk when the rain came down like silver needles, so she put her old shawl over her head and jumped over the puddles as well as she could. By the time she reached the clearing where she knew her father had been working, the rain had stopped and the sun was out. There she saw the axe, fixed in the stump of a tree. On the handle perched two snow-white doves, who were wet and shivering with cold. 'Coo-coo-roo!' cooed the doves unhappily. 'Coo-coo-roo!'

'You poor little birds!' said Mariette, and she dried their feathers with her shawl and warmed them between her hands. Then she fed them with the crust she had kept to cheer herself on her long walk home. When they had pecked up every crumb, a little dwarf, dressed all in yellow, stepped from behind a bush, and with a whirr of white wings the doves flew on to his shoulders, cooing excitedly in his pointed

73

ears. 'Coo-coo-roo!' they cried. 'Coo-coo-roo!'

The little man listened, nodding from time to time, and when they had finished he said to Mariette, 'What can I give you as a reward for your kindness to my doves?'

'But I want no reward,' she replied.

'Maybe,' said the yellow dwarf. 'But my doves and I would like to give you something. What shall it be, my dear?'

Mariette thought the little man

74

looked as poor as she was herself, and could ill afford to give her anything. But, as she did not want to hurt his feelings, she looked hurriedly round and said, after a pause, 'I should like – a wreath of wild roses!'

With surprising speed, the yellow dwarf picked some strands of the wild roses which hung from the branches of a bush, and with strange flickering movements of his hands wove them into a wreath and held it out to her.

75

'How beautiful!' said Mariette, holding it up.

'It's no ordinary wreath,' said the dwarf. 'Look closely, my dear.'

Then Mariette saw that, perched among the flowers, were dozens of tiny blue birds, no bigger than her thimble.

'Sing, little blue birds! Sing!' cried the dwarf, and the tiny creatures lifted up their golden bills and sang as sweetly as the nightingale when the moon is full.

Mariette laughed with pleasure,

76

and put the wreath on her head. Then she thanked the yellow dwarf, put the axe over her shoulder and went skipping home. And the wreath sang to her all the way, so that it seemed no distance at all.

When at last she reached the woodcutter's hut, and Maria saw the rosy wreath and heard the sweet singing of the tiny birds, she said, '*I* want a wreath that sings!' And she grabbed the wreath and put it on. But no sooner had she settled it on her tousled hair than the wild roses began to fade and drop their pink petals, while the little birds turned to buzzing bluebottles.

'It's a *horrid* wreath!' grumbled Maria, pulling it off her head and flinging it on the floor. 'I shall go to the forest myself, and I expect the yellow dwarf will give me something much more grand.' And, after kicking the faded wreath into a corner, off she went. But when Mariette picked up the wreath and put it on again, at once the drooping roses lifted their heads and bloomed, and the bluebottles ceased their buzzing and became little singing blue birds again.

When Maria reached the clearing in the forest, she was even more bad-tempered than usual, for she had borrowed Mariette's Sunday shoes, and they were much too tight. When she saw the white doves perched upon the tree stump, she cried, 'Get away, you stupid creatures! *I* want to sit there!' And she flapped them away and sat down. Then she kicked off her tight

shoes and waggled her ugly great toes and began to eat a slab of plum cake she had brought with her.

The doves looked on with their bright eyes and hopped round expectantly, but, instead of crumbs, Maria threw first one shoe and then the other at the poor birds, crying as she did so, 'Do you think I have carried a great heavy piece of

cake all this way just to
feed a lot of silly
birds? Get away,
you greedy guzzlers!'
And the doves flew sadly
away.

'I wish that dwarf would hurry
up,' went on Maria. 'I want my
reward.'

'And you shall have your
reward!' said the yellow dwarf,
stepping suddenly from behind a
tree. 'I saw it all. "Greedy guzzlers"
you called my doves, so from now

81

on those shall be the only words you can say!'

Maria thought of all kinds of rude things to say to him in reply, but it was no use. The only words that came from her lips were – 'Greedy guzzlers!'

When she reached home, she gargled and rubbed her throat till it was sore both inside and out, but it made no difference; she could still only say 'Greedy guzzlers!'

Now, the fame of the wreath that sang, and the beauty of the girl

who wore it, soon spread abroad,
and who should come to see for
himself, one day, but the king's son.
As soon as he saw Mariette's lovely
face he fell in love with her and
asked her to be his wife. They were
married in the great cathedral and
all the choir fell silent at the singing
of the little blue birds, and the
carved saints turned their stone
heads to listen.

★

You would expect me to say that
they both lived happily ever after.

And so they would have done if it had not been for Maria, who was eaten up with jealousy. Although all she could still *say* was 'Greedy guzzlers!' she *thought* to herself, 'Why should Mariette live in a King's palace, and wear a golden gown, while I live in a poor hut, in nothing but rags?' And she went on thinking this until a wicked plan came into her head. She had often been told by her father how she and Mariette had once been so alike. Supposing she brushed her hair and tried really hard to look pleasant, could she make herself look as pretty as Mariette? She fetched her sister's hairbrush, and, standing in front of the little cracked mirror, which was all she had, she brushed and brushed until, gradually, the dust of weeks came away and her hair began to shine almost as brightly as Mariette's did. Next, she tried looking pleasant. This was a great deal harder. But she smirked and ogled at herself in the mirror until her mouth began to turn up at the corners, and only if you looked closely could you see the crosspatch wrinkles. And at last she really did begin to look like Mariette.

Then she ran as fast as she could to the palace. When she saw Mariette feeding the peacocks on the terrace, the sight of the splendour in which her sister now lived caused Maria to look for a moment as cross as she had ever done, so that Mariette had no difficulty recognizing her. She was

86

delighted to see her again and loaded her with presents.

Then she asked her what she would like most to do. Just remembering in time not to speak, Maria made signs that there was nothing she would like better on such a hot day than to bathe. Mariette agreed. And so they made their way to the palace lake, which lay in the middle of trees. But no sooner had Mariette slipped off her golden gown than Maria took her by the shoulders and pushed her in

87

the water. Then she picked up the singing wreath, and threw it after her. And both Mariette and the wreath sank beneath the still water of the lake. Twittering sadly, the blue birds flew away.

Then Maria crowed with glee and, after changing her ragged skirt for Mariette's golden gown, she smoothed her hair, smirking cheerfully, made her way to the palace, pushing rudely past the servants and sometimes, forgetting that she must hold her tongue, calling the courtiers 'greedy guzzlers', to their great surprise.

When the prince found that though his princess looked much the same as usual her manners had become rude and rough, he was sadly troubled. 'What is the matter, my dear?' he asked. 'And why will you not speak to me? Are you ill?'

But Maria knew better than to try to answer. So the prince sent for the wisest doctors in the land. But they could find no cure for her silence or her rude, rough behaviour. All she would do was eat and throw things at the servants.

Weeks went by, and the prince grew pale and thin, for he had loved his gentle wife. One day, as he sat silent in his garden, he thought he saw a cloud of tiny blue butterflies, which hovered over the rosebush beneath which he was sitting.

Suddenly, they began to sing – as sweetly as the nightingale when the moon is full. Now butterflies do not sing, so the prince started up and recognized at once the little blue birds. 'Tell me,' he said, 'What has happened to the singing wreath? And what can I do to change my princess back to the gentle wife I loved so well?'

All at once, the blue birds darted off like dragonflies, and the prince followed. They led him to the lake, where they hovered over the water as though they were waiting for something, and, as he watched, he saw the water stir and dimple and, through a ring of shining ripples, rose the real princess, with the wreath upon her head.

'Dear husband!' cried Mariette. 'My jealous sister pushed me into

the lake and threw the wreath after me. She did not know that as long as I wear it I can live an enchanted life beneath the water.'

'She looks like you, and wears your clothes, but there the likeness ends,' said the prince. 'Dear wife, what can I do to break this watery spell and bring you back again?'

'Listen well, my dear,' replied Mariette. 'For I must return to the mud and ooze at the bottom of the lake. When I sink once more beneath the water, you will find the

93

singing wreath floating on the surface. Take it quickly to the palace and put it on the head of my cruel sister, and you will see her as she really is.'

'What then?' asked the prince.

'If you wish to save me,' said Mariette, 'before the sun sets you must dive to the bottom of the lake. There, in the mud, you will see a hideous great slug. Take it in your arms and carry it to the shore. Remember, whatever it may turn into, hold it fast, or you will never

94

see me again. Above all, make haste. Once the sun has set I can live no longer under the water without the singing wreath.'

As she spoke, Mariette sank once more into the lake. Only the ripples showed where she had been. And there, on the surface, floated the singing wreath. It drifted to the bank where the prince stood. He took it up, and the tiny blue birds settled among the roses, singing joyfully. Then he hurried to the palace, and who should come to meet him but Maria, elbowing her way through the courtiers. Before she could prevent him, he put the wreath on her head. At once, the roses began to droop, and when Maria saw their fading petals falling to the ground, and heard the singing of the blue birds turn to the buzzing of angry bluebottles she was so furious that her mouth turned down at the corners, and all the crosspatch wrinkles creased her face again so that she looked as ugly as she had ever done. By the prince's horrified face she realized that she had been discovered, and, flinging the wreath on the floor, she turned and fled for her life and was never seen again.

Then the prince saw that the rim of the sun was just beginning to sink behind a bank of purple cloud, and he ran to the lake as fast as he could go. By the time he came to the wood, a quarter of the sun had sunk behind the cloud. When he reached the lake and dived into the water, only half the crimson circle could be seen.

Down, down he went, to the bottom of the lake, and there, as Mariette had said, he found a hideous great slug. Steeling himself to touch the slimy thing, he shut his eyes and, clasping it in his arms, fought his way up again. Suddenly, he found he was holding not a slug, but a serpent, whose coils twisted themselves round him in such a grip he could scarcely move.

But he held it fast. Just as he reached the surface the serpent changed into a great bird, whose

98

wings were made of iron and whose beak was of steel, with which it attacked the prince. But still he held it fast and, as he stumbled ashore, the spell was broken, the bird was gone, and in its place was his own dear wife, Mariette. And at that very minute the last of the sun disappeared behind the purple cloud.

Then Mariette and the prince walked back to the palace hand in hand, in great joy and contentment.

And, this time, they really *did* live happily ever after.

The Princess's New Nose

Anna Wilson

Princess Precious was a proud princess, and she was especially proud of her teeny-weeny, tiny little nose. It was a nose covered in just enough little freckles to set off its perfect prettiness. It was a nose that turned up at the end just enough to be described as 'cute' rather than 'ski jump'. And, most importantly, it was a nose that was just big enough to enable the princess to look down it at people whose profiles were not quite so perfect.

'My beauty is extraordinary – it's as plain as the noses on their faces,' she sighed.

Everywhere that Princess Precious went, she was worshipped for her perfect nose. Her courtiers bowed low as she swept through the palace grounds. They muttered:

'Good morning, Your Nosiness.'

'Bless you, Your Hooterness.'

'Good day, Your High Conkness.'

Now, this might sound incredibly rude to you or me, but it was music to Princess Precious's ears (not to mention her nose).

And so, day after day, she rode through her kingdom, nose in the air.

'Oooo!' she heard as she passed through the villages.

'Aaah!' cried the crowds as she cantered through the towns.

Simply no one could believe how utterly, ravishingly beautiful their princess was. She was perfect. Well, almost.

You see, when Princess Precious wasn't parading her prettiness all over the country, the thing she liked doing best was sticking her perfect

103

nose into other people's business. She liked to know what was going on in her kingdom, and was top-notch at sniffing out a scandal.

For example, when the prime minister forgot to change his socks before going into parliament, the princess was the first to pick up the scent – and she made sure that everyone else got wind of it too. She held her snooty snout between delicate finger and delicate thumb and cried out, 'PHEW! Papa darling, what's that AWFUL cheesy whiff?'

To which the king responded, sounding quite shamefaced, 'I say, PM old thing. There is rather a hum of the old gorgonzola around today. Go and change your socks before we start, eh old boy?'

The prime minister was, not surprisingly, none too pleased.

Then there was the time the palace priest overslept and hadn't had a chance to wash. Well, the princess was the first to broadcast the evidence, rather tactlessly: 'POO-EY! Papa dear, that aroma of boiled cabbage is putting me off my prayers!'

To which the king responded, sounding quite embarrassed, 'The thing is, Father Whatsyername old chum, it is rather fruity in here this morning. Go and have a quick splash in the font before we start, eh?'

The priest was, understandably, slightly upset.

And then, of course, there was the occasion when the cook had greedily polished off all the garlic bread in secret before serving supper. Guess who spilled the beans on him?

'YEUCK! Don't come so close, Cook! No wonder you don't have a girlfriend. No one in their right minds would kiss a gruesome garlic-flavoured geek!'

To which everyone responded by sniggering rather unkindly into their gold-edged napkins.

The cook was, quite naturally, a bit put out.

As you can imagine, the palace personnel became more than a little peeved at the princess's nosiness, and they held a meeting to discuss what they could do to put a stop to it.

'Her beauty might be the pride of the kingdom, but it sure gets up my nose,' muttered the prime minister.

108

'Mmm,' agreed the priest. 'That nose knows too much.'

'She definitely puts my nose out of joint,' grumbled the cook. 'We need a plan that'll teach her a lesson once and for all. I know! How about putting pepper in her hot chocolate?' He sniggered. 'She'd be so busy sneezing that she wouldn't have a minute to be meddlesome!'

'No – it wouldn't work. She'd be sure to sniff out the culprit,' said the prime minister. 'I know! We could

109

pass a law against having a nose smaller than mine, and then we could lock her up—'

'We'd all end up in prison then,' smirked the priest. The prime minister's nose was rather larger than the average turnip, after all. 'No, what we need is a miracle . . .' His eyes lit up. 'That's it!' he cried. 'We need Nigella Fudge!'

'Oh dear, he's finally flipped,' whispered the prime minister, who was feeling mightily miffed at the priest's comment on his conk.

110

'No, no, no – Nigella Fudge – the Fairy Godmother,' explained the priest. 'Don't any of you remember the royal christening?'

The prime minister and the cook thought back. Ten years ago, when the perfect pink parcel that was Princess Precious had been delivered to the palace, the priest had performed the christening ceremony. There hadn't been many fairies still in active service at the time, but the three that were left in the kingdom agreed to come.

111

There was Mirabella, who granted the princess good health.

There was Donnatella, who granted the princess great wealth.

And then there was Nigella, who granted the princess her stupendous snout.

'Yes, yes, we remember now,' chorused the prime minister and the cook together.

'But so what?' said the PM huffily. 'What use is Nigella to us in our present dilemma?' (He liked to use big words, as it made him sound so very important.)

'Well, Nigella gave the princess her nose, so only she can undo all the trouble it's caused,' the priest explained slowly. He wasn't fooled by the PM's long words – he'd always known the PM was a blithering idiot.

'Hallelujah!' cried the cook, showing the priest he appreciated his cleverness. 'But where is Nigella these days?' he sighed, slumping back into his chair.

'In retirement,' said the priest.

113

'The royal christening was her last official engagement.'

It was true Nigella didn't do much work these days. In fact, she spent most of her time conjuring up cakes and scoffing the lot. She was more interested in the state of her larder than in the state of the kingdom.

'There's nothing for it: we'll have to tempt her back into service,' said the prime minister. 'And, Cook – you are definitely the man for the job.'

114

The cook beamed and started writing a long shopping list right away.

That afternoon, the cook sent the prime minister and the priest out shopping. They bought all the sugar, eggs, flour, cocoa and chocolate buttons in the kingdom. The cook locked himself away and concocted and confected all through the night. He didn't sleep, he didn't eat – he didn't even lick the bowl.

Finally the kitchen door opened,

and the cook emerged in a cloud of flour and frosting, holding the most enormous chocolate cake ever seen. Its crowning glory was the decoration: NIGELLA, spelled out in tiny specks of chocolate-flavoured gold leaf.

'It's done,' he announced. 'Now all we have to do is wait.'

No sooner had the cook spoken than there was a shower of hundreds and thousands and a loud THUD! The cake collapsed under the impact of a very heavy object – and an atrocious apparition of frothy pink and sparkly wings emerged from the mess.

'NIGELLA FUDGE!' cried the priest and the PM.

'You called?' she trilled, between mouthfuls of cake and icing.

117

'Mfffuglled!' gurgled the cook, who was buried beneath the fairy and the frosting.

The prime minister helped the cook to dust himself down while the priest explained the princess's bad behaviour.

'Is there any more cake?' asked Nigella.

'As much as you like, if you'll agree to help us,' puffed the cook and he told Nigella the plan.

'Done! I was getting tired of my own recipes anyway,' smiled the fairy. 'Your wish, as I used to say, is my command.' And she disappeared in a flash of pink sugar flowers.

What the plotters in the kitchen did not know was that Princess Precious had been watching all these sugary shenanigans through the keyhole! Her super sense of smell had helped her to sniff out all the sugar in the air, and she'd followed her nose to find out what was going on.

'So Cook is baking again – *it*

119

must be for a party!' she thought to herself. 'And he's even invited one of my fairy godmothers! How sweet of him – he's not such a geek after all. I must go and get ready.'

The princess was so vain that she was sure the cake could only be for her.

So she went to her room to choose her fanciest frock for the occasion and looked into the mirror, preening and pouting.

'Mirror, mirror, on the wall, whose nose is the fairest of them

120

all?' she simpered at her reflection.

Unfortunately the mirror wasn't magic, and Princess Precious felt rather foolish when she realized she wasn't alone.

'Talking to yourself, dearie?' cooed Nigella, who had appeared on a cloud of meringue. 'A sure sign that all is not well. And what's all this I hear about your naughty nosiness and silly snootiness? It's time Aunty Nigella taught you a lesson.'

And with a swish and a swoosh of Nigella's wand, a large lump of red icing shot out and landed on the princess's nose. It stuck fast. Princess Precious was utterly horrified.

'Nosy? Snooty? What do you mean?' shrieked the princess. 'And what have you done to my beautiful nose?'

122

She tugged hard at the red blob of icing, but it would not budge.

'Everyone in the kingdom is fed up with you looking down your nose at them and listening in on all their business,' explained the fairy, 'so I've decided to give you a new nose.'

And with that Nigella Fudge disappeared, leaving a trail of dolly mixtures behind her.

'She's wrong!' cried the princess. 'Everyone loves me! I am beautiful. I am beloved. I am the best!'

After shedding a few icing-stained

tears, Princess Precious pulled herself together. She decided to use her ill-won disguise to ride out into the kingdom and listen in on her subjects. Then she would find out what they really thought of her.

'Let's see whether Nigella is right. After all, no one will recognize me with this nasty new nose,' she reasoned.

Princess Precious was right: no one did recognize her. And this is what they were saying about her:

'That princess of ours . . .'

grumbled one woman. 'Precious by name and precious by nature, if you ask me.'

'Who does she think she is anyway? Sticking her nose into our affairs,' agreed another.

'She might be beautiful, but her manners stink!' cried someone else.

Poor Precious had heard enough. She burst into tears and sped off home.

Once through the palace gates, the princess raced to the kitchen and pushed open the doors, sobbing and sniffing. The prime minister, the cook and the priest were having a cup of tea and some fairy fudge fingers with Nigella.

'All right! All right! You *were* right! I am nosy and nasty and nobody likes me!' cried the princess, wiping tears from her icing-stained face.

The prime minister, the cook, the priest and Nigella were shocked to see Precious in such a state.

'Dry your eyes, dearie,' Nigella cooed. 'If you promise to be a good

126

girl, we can sort this mess out.'

Precious gulped, nodded, and promised. 'I'll never be nosy or nasty again,' she whispered, 'if only I can have my nose back.'

So Nigella waved her wand, the princess's prettiness was restored, and Precious declared the next day a national holiday. Then she asked Nigella and the cook to bake a chocolate cake in the shape of the palace and she held a party for the whole kingdom as an apology for her awfulness.

127

'Three cheers for Nigella!'
chorused the princess and the palace
personnel.

'Ah!' The fairy smiled, sniffing the

sugar-filled air, and planting a kiss on Precious's beautiful button nose. 'What an appetising aroma – the sweet smell of success!'

Cinderella Rap

Tony Mitton

I'm gonna tell a story
'bout a girl I know.
The whole thing happened
a long time ago.
She lived with her stepmother
(cruel and mean)
and the nastiest sisters

there ever been.
Now these two sisters
and that mean old mum,
they treated Cinderella
like she was dumb.
They fed her on scraps,
gave her rags to wear.

131

They bossed her about

and it just wasn't fair.

They got her to clean

and they made her cook,

but they hardly ever gave her

a word or a look

except to say,

'Hey there, Sis, come here . . .

Do this and do that

and now – disappear!'

And that's about the way

her life went by

with hardly the time

for a sob or a sigh.

Until one day

with a RAT-TAT-TAT

a golden invitation card

dropped on the mat.

Cinderella listened

while Stepma read,

and these are the words
that the invite said:
'Prince Charming has reached
that time in life
when a prince oughta settle down
and find a wife.
And if the girl he wants
agrees and says "Yes!"
then she's gonna be
our new princess.
So if you wanna sit
on a royal throne,
don't stay at home
watching TV alone.

134

Dress yourself up
in your very best frock
and come to the palace
at eight o'clock.
Make sure that you get here.
Don't miss this chance.
"It could BE YOU!"
at the Engagement Dance.'
'Oh, Mama, dear Mama,'
said Sister One,
'I'll go in my red dress.
This sounds like fun.'
'Oh, yes, dear Mama,'
said Sister Two,

'I'll dye my hair pink
and go in blue.'
'Oh, Mama, please Mama,'
said young Cinderella,
'I guess Prince Charming
is a real nice fella.
I know that a prince
wouldn't want to marry me,
but maybe, please, Mama,
I could just go see . . . ?'
'Well, really, Cinderella,
it's not for you.
You haven't the time,
you've work to do.

We need to get ready.

We want to look nice.

Get back to your kitchen –

I won't tell you twice.'

The evening came round

in no time at all

and everyone went

to the royal ball.

So Cinderella wept

as she did the dirty dishes,

but while she washed up

she dreamed up wishes.

'I wish I could go to the royal

   ball,

I wish I could be the fairest one
    of all,
I wish I could wear a wonderful
    dress,
I wish I could be that new
    princess.'
'OK, honey,'
said a real sweet voice.
'High-fashion dress
and a white Rolls-Royce?
It ain't no trouble
to a mama like me.
I got the magic.
Just watch and see!'

And there, right in front of her,

Cinderella saw

a big fairy mama

at the kitchen door.

'I'll fix your wishes, honey,

don't you worry.

But there ain't much time,

so the word is – hurry!'

She snatched a dirty saucepan

and flung it at a rat,

cried, 'ALA KAZAM!'

and that was that:

the rat turned chauffeur,

the saucepan shone clean

and stretched itself into

a long limousine.

And Cinderella stood there

in a beautiful gown.

'Driver!' said the mama,

'Take her to town.

But make sure you're back

before midnight's here,

140

cos all this magic's
gonna disappear.'
Well, telling it quickly,
and telling it straight
Cinderella went
and she stayed till late.
She danced with the prince
and her wish came true.
He smiled and he said,
'Cindie, baby, it's you . . .'
They stopped for a burger
and a bubbly drink,
when Cinderella's digital
began to twink.

Cinderella vanished,

and all the prince found

was a small glass sneaker

lying on the ground.

But the prince wasn't beaten.

He gave a command

to drive that sneaker

all around the land.

And when they found the foot

that glass sneaker fit,

well, the girl on the end,

why – she had to be it.

Well, let me reassure you

that it didn't take long,

142

For, after all, a magic sneaker
can't go wrong.

Everyone tried it.
Everybody failed.
The first sister wept
and the second one wailed.
But Cinderella's foot fit
neat as a glove,
and that was the start
of a sole-ful love.

So that's how Cinderella

got to get her wishes –

a life at the palace

and no more dishes.

(Except that the prince

is a bit of a dish.

He's the hunkiest guy

that a girl could wish.)

But back at home her sisters

are down on all fours,

sweeping up the dust

and polishing the floors.

And Stepma's had to learn

to sew and to mend,

so she can stitch the story up –
this is the end.

The Reluctant Dragon and the Wilful Princess

William Raeper

Reginald lolled back and puffed out his scaly chest. 'Oh – oh – umm!' he yawned, licking his hard, shiny lips. 'Such a delicious day.'

The daisies were drowsy in the heat, their faces pointed sleepily

towards the sun, and nearby a careless brook tinkled over a myriad of coloured pebbles. Reginald pared a solitary claw and rolled his large bulging eyes round in his head.

Sleep had refreshed his limbs and the scents of summer filled his smoky nostrils.

'This is the life!' he hummed to himself. 'This is the Life!' and a little shower of sparks tumbled from his mouth on to the grass.

Reginald was, you see, a dragon. Not a dragon of the old school who burned up villages and terrorized young maidens, but a dragon of the new school who did nothing at all. He practised a little flying before dinner perhaps, or roasted the occasional animal, but he attempted nothing too strenuous — or barbaric. He lived in the well of a pleasant valley that was pleasantly warm in summer and pleasantly cool in winter. He had a cave to snuggle in and a hoard of treasure to guard. He was completely and peacefully content, if pricked at times by an uncomfortable feeling of boredom. Reginald had lived in the valley longer than even he could remember, and although there had been a time when he had been fierce – gushing fire all over helpless men and innocent forests – he had not done anything of that kind for hundreds of years.

'I could lie here forever,' thought Reginald dreamily to himself. 'The sunlight is very like nectar.' And plucking a daisy (which had been minding its own business) in one shiny claw, Reginald set himself to contemplate the beauties of nature for a while.

He had just wrinkled his eyes shut, and a thin column of smoke was rising from his nose in a doze, when he awoke with a start to find himself covered by a huge black shadow. Reginald shivered. Flapping towards him out of the west, he saw, etched against the glassy sky, the form and outline of another dragon.

'Oh dear,' thought Reginald. 'I do hope this doesn't mean trouble.' But trouble it undoubtedly was.

The dragon swooped round the valley once in a long extended circle and, with a few flaps of his

151

leathery wings, alighted on the grass near Reginald. Instantly it burst into flames.

'Oh dear,' murmured Reginald, feeling trouble, or rather Trouble with a capital 'T', growing nearer every moment. He squirmed like a naughty schoolboy about to be faced with a stern headmaster.

The dragon was larger than Reginald and had scales of burnished copper. Two sulphurous clouds of smoke rose thickly from his nostrils. His eyes were the colour

152

of honey and his claws shone like polished brass.

'Reginald,' he boomed, his voice rumbling like distant thunder.

'Yes?' said Reginald weakly. 'How – uh – nice to see you again. When was the last time we met?' He fingered the daisy he was holding nervously.

'Do you know why I have come?' frowned the copper dragon majestically.

'No – not really,' stammered Reginald. He shrugged his scaly

153

shoulders and the row of fins on his long, sinuous back trembled.

'We're very disappointed with you – very!' said the copper dragon, getting down to business right away. His name was Bertram, and in dragon circles he was extremely high up and official. Reginald coiled up and looked glum. He shook his head appealingly and helplessly.

'You were given this portion of land to terrorize and you do nothing! Why, you're a laughing stock! No one in good dragon society would dare to receive you.'

Reginald could not remember the last time he had bothered to approach good dragon society, but he kept his mountainous, jagged teeth clamped shut on his thick jewel-encrusted tongue and said nothing.

'When was the last time you terrorized a maiden?'

Reginald said nothing.

'When was the last time you rained down fire on a village?'

Reginald said nothing.

155

'It's hopeless! Hopeless! Don't you understand? We're in the business of control. Unless we keep the men down, think what will happen! If you don't burn the villages to the south, the men will explore, advance, choke and cut down the forest. If you don't terrorize a few maidens, those humans will grow cocky and think they rule the roost. Is that what you want to happen?'

Reginald shook his head vigorously.

'No, of course not,' continued

Bertram. 'You have an important job to do, a tradition to keep up. You ought to be proud of these things and not disgrace them. What would your father have said? I remember him in the old days – a hundred thousand knights extinguished in one gush of flame – now *that* was something to see.' Bertram's honey eyes burned excitedly at the memory.

'But you,' he rumbled accusingly, 'if you don't buck up, you'll have your licence revoked, and you know what that means!'

Reginald searched the cavern of his brain. It was big and did not contain much information. He wrinkled his snout. 'Remind me,' he said feebly.

'Your fire will be put out and you'll be condemned to lie on an ice floe near the North Pole for the rest of your life.'

Reginald shuddered. He never could abide fish and seals and other creatures from the sea – slimy, furry things tasting of salt. 'Ugh!' he said.

158

'Now,' said Bertram, 'I want to see your contract. Where is it?'

'My contract?' breathed Reginald. 'It's in there, I think.' He pointed with a curved claw at the squashed-circle mouth of his cave.

'Go and get it then,' hissed Bertram impatiently. 'Honestly, you haven't a clue. When robbers came to steal your treasure you didn't even wake up!'

'I was tired,' said Reginald. 'Besides, they didn't take much.'

'As much as they could carry

159

probably,' growled Bertram. 'Do you want people to laugh at dragons?' he said, as though the idea was more chilling than the ice floe Reginald might be condemned to lie on. Dragons are fairly humourless creatures, but then they have fairly humourless jobs.

Reginald lumbered into his cave, leaving only four feet of his pointed tail thrashing about in the sunlight. There was a clink and a rumble and the crash of pots and pans and chalices and breastplates from the darkness within. Finally Reginald's snout reappeared, his eyes as wide and as round as dinner plates. In one claw he grasped a rolled, yellowed parchment tied up with a crimson ribbon.

'I found it,' said Reginald cheerfully. 'The place is a bit of a mess, though.'

'Congratulations,' said Bertram dryly, taking the scroll from him. He unrolled it with one claw, pinning the parchment to the ground with the other. The

161

parchment was written impressively in dragon runes painted in the old style.

'You see,' said Bertram.

'What?' said Reginald.

'It says here. Look.'

Reginald squinted and twisted his long back.

'One,' said Bertram, 'I hereby undertake to fulfil my duties as a dragon in the region allotted to me. Two: I will terrorize maidens whenever possible. Three: I will guard what treasure I can amass jealously and loyally with loss of life and limb to anyone who may try to steal it. Four: I will be fearsome and firesome at all times. Five . . .'

Bertram read on and on till he came to number twenty-nine. Twenty-nine! Bertram's voice marched relentlessly through all twenty-nine articles of the Dragons' Code, and as he read Reginald sat looking away in shame, tapping his claws on the grass. He knew he had not kept one of them. Bertram knew he had not kept one. The trouble was, Reginald did not want to spend his time burning and terrorizing. Burning and terrorizing bored him to bits. But the thought of being chained to an ice floe resolved him to try – for a little while, at least.

'What do you say to that then – eh?' grated Bertram. Small tongues of fire fringed his lips.

But there was nothing, nothing Reginald could say. He wished Bertram would spread his wings and leave him in peace.

164

'You have three months,' warned Bertram. 'And then I'll be back. If you haven't improved your performance by then there'll be a price to pay. They say it's cold up at the North Pole at this time of the year.' Bertram smiled grimly, revealing two rows of diamond teeth. Spreading out his wide wings, he gave one, two, three flaps and lifted a few inches off the ground. 'Mind what I say. The Dragon Council will be watching you from now on.'

Reginald watched Bertram's bulk recede with a mournful expression on his face, till Bertram was only a dot on the horizon.

'What to do? What to do?' thought Reginald anxiously. But after all that unpleasant excitement he really and most truly thought he deserved a rest.

'Later,' he purred, squeezing into a comfortable position. 'I'll think about it later.' And he fell asleep.

For the first week after Bertram's visit Reginald did nothing but sleep and worry. He slept more than he worried, as he found sleep to be a good solution to the problems he faced when he was awake. He knew his weak resolution would not carry him far – it hardly carried him to the end of the valley. For a couple of days he tried scouting around. Once he tried blasting a tree, but he was so out of practice that he only singed its leaves and swallowed most of his own fire by mistake, which made him feel quite ill. He was glad no one had caught sight of him making this blunder and fled the scene with embarrassment, leaving the barely smoking tree wondering what had happened to it.

His dread of the ice floe began to wane after this disaster. He played in his mind with the words Bertram had spoken to him, trying to take the sting out of them, and at last he managed to convince himself that the copper dragon probably had not meant what he had said. Reginald was one of those creatures who, being so safe and secure in their own little nests and leading such pleasant trouble-free lives, believe nothing bad can happen to them.

He received a rude jolt, however, when a letter from Bertram arrived:

Dear Reginald,

I hope you have taken my words to heart. The Council meets at the end of August to decide on your future. I shall be back to visit you some time before then. Jonathan has won the maiden-terrorizing cup again this year for the third time running. Sickening,

169

isn't it! I enclose a picture of an ice floe to remind you what will happen to you if you don't shake yourself up a bit.

Yours with best wishes,

Bertram

'Oh, the beast,' howled Reginald. 'Ruining my life like this!' And he had a good half-hour's malice, thinking of what he would like to do to Bertram. It must have been good exercise for him since, for the first time in years, he soared up into

170

the sky and flapped off to where the villages of men had lain undisturbed for generations.

A little to the north and a little to the west of where Reginald lived in his pleasant valley, there was a castle, and in this castle lived Princess Rosie, a wilful king's daughter. That is, *she* was wilful. The king, a man as meek as a mole, preferred paperwork to people. He had a chancellor who dealt with his subjects and gave in to his daughter wherever possible.

He did, however, have plans. Rosie was sixteen, too old for a nurse and too young for a husband. She had burning, spark-filled eyes, red flaming hair and freckles. And a temper. What a temper! That morning she had fairly screamed at

her nurse, 'I am not a child! I am not!' thus proving how much of a child she still was. Against the nurse's orders, she rode away on her pony, Quartermaine – on her own. The poor nurse wrung her hands and sobbed into her rocking chair. Soon the garment she was knitting was soaked right through and dripped down on to the floor.

Rosie was really in a temper because rumours had fluttered to her ears about her father's plans for her. There lived, two seas away from them, her uncle and aunt and cousin. Her cousin was a pimply, gangly youth called Prince Humphrey. As a child the prince had loved to climb trees, and when he was very young had acquired the nickname 'Squirrel', which had stuck. The rumour that the princess heard, whispered to her by her nurse who never could keep a secret, was that she was to be presented to Prince Squirrel as a possible bride. Bride! She had scarcely laid aside her hoop and

skipping rope. Princess Rosie stewed in her anger for days, clutching her pillow over her face and squealing, 'Never. Never. Never. Never will I marry that spotty pudding! He can't even ride a horse straight!'

So she had ridden away, over the river and through the meadow, taken a wrong turning, tumbled off her horse and found herself alone and lost. Lost! She rubbed her head. There was a painful bump rising gently under her fingers. It was all too much. Too much! She glanced

175

around, still sprawled in the long grass. There was not one hoof-nail of Quartermaine to be seen.

'When I get hold of that horse . . .' she thought angrily, twisting her hands together. But she knew, sadly, that she was where she was through her own fault. 'I suppose I was riding him too hard – and not looking where I was going.'

It so happened that Reginald, still smouldering from Bertram's letter, was scouting around over the place where Rosie sat. He was looking for

176

someone to terrorize. Anyone would do, so long as they were not too big and strong. Tree-burning had not been a success so, scoring Article One off the list, he had decided to have a go at Article Two and go back to Article One later on when he felt more capable. Dragons are keen-eyed and Reginald spotted Rosie's riding breeches from high up in the air. He was so high up he seemed to her only the outline of a distant bird.

'Aha!' thought Reginald to himself. 'Prey! Oh – goody! Now, is

she quite alone?' He checked, and
to his satisfaction saw there was no
other human being near her.

'Foolish girl,' he mumbled and,
pointing his snout earthwards,
turned his body into a dive. Rosie
heard the struggle of wings in the
air above her and, looking up, saw
Reginald's glittering body snake its
way down to the ground in front of
her. The dragon reared up on his
hind legs, rattled his wings, shook
his podgy claws and roared. Rosie
looked at him . . . well . . . rather

as she would have done at her father if he had dressed up in a silly suit and done childish party tricks. Disdainful – yes. Amazed – yes. Disgusted – slightly. Afraid – no.

'What do you want?' she said, not turning a hair, for princesses rarely turn one in any situation. 'I'm lost. Maybe you can help me find my way back.'

'Eeargh – argh – harrgh – er!' roared Reginald, and he set fire to a hawthorn bush with two gobs of flame.

'Nnyeeargh – ghghgh – gh!'
Reginald's eyes opened, his nostrils
contracted and he roared, roared
with all his might. The trees shook.
The grasses quivered . . . and . . .
and . . . he dissolved into a fit of
coughing that racked his massive
stomach.

'It's no use,' he said, 'no use at
all. You're not frightened, are you?'
he complained disappointedly.

'No, not at all,' returned Rosie.
'Should I be?'

'Yes, yes, YES!' wailed Reginald,

sprouting two feathers of white
smoke out of his nostrils.

'Why didn't you say?'

'I'm not supposed to say. You're
supposed to tremble naturally.'
Reginald was feeling quite offish.
He could be huffy when he liked.

Rosie, looking at his ridiculous
bulk and listening to his petulant
voice, began to giggle. She made a
little stuttering noise. Then her body
shook. Then tears ran down her
cheeks. Then she laughed out loud.
Reginald ground his teeth together,

181

sullen and hurt. 'When you've quite finished,' he interrupted, peeved, 'I'm going to carry you off to my lair.'

'Fine,' said Rosie, equal to anything Reginald might say. 'But don't drop me or I shall never forgive you.'

Reginald picked up Rosie in his two claws and set her on his back. Her hands clasped the toughest of his pointed fins. It was the one nearest his neck. With one, two, three flaps of his wings, Reginald hovered a few inches off the ground and then rose slowly above the trees. Beneath them the valley spread out in a patchwork shape: woods and fields and rivers. In a great arc, up above tufts of combed-out cloud and down again, Reginald soared and fell. If on the earth he was cumbersome and heavy, in the air he was as light as a feather, as sleek as a dolphin and as graceful as a bird. He was as particular about his flying as a great pianist is about his playing.

183

Reginald knew that flying was the
one thing he was especially good at
and he wanted to impress Rosie.

When they landed by the mouth
of Reginald's cave Rosie was

beaming, her cheeks glowing and her eyes shining. 'That was so good,' she said. 'You will take me up again, won't you?' She straightened her mouth into an appealing line.

Reginald despaired. For a terrorization this was not going well at all. He thought of holding her to ransom and swapping her for a few gold cups to build up his pile of treasure, but had to decide against this idea as kidnapping and ransom were not part of the Dragon's Code of Ethics. Reginald rubbed his claws together and pushed his snout into Rosie's face.

'Would you like some tea?' he asked.

'That would be lovely,' said Rosie.

And they had a lovely afternoon together. That was the problem. As they munched buns and sticky cake Reginald was haunted by the thoughts of the ice floe waiting for him at the North Pole. Both his ears dropped and he looked disgruntled.

'What's the matter?' asked Rosie, her mouth full of sticky cake.

Reginald heaved his shoulders and gave a sigh. Three sparks tumbled from his lips. Terrorization had been a failure. He told Rosie everything. He told her what a disgrace he was to dragonkind and about what the Dragon Council thought of him and about what he had to do for them and about what would happen to him if he didn't.

'You poor thing,' sympathized Rosie. 'How beastly. But

187

bureaucrats are always the same. Daddy says so.' And she told Reginald about how she had heard her father planned to marry her to Prince Humphrey and how she never would and how she had run away, fallen off her horse and found herself lost.

'A fine pair we are,' she said, and gave a wry smile. 'We can't seem to please anybody.'

By the time they had finished talking to each other it was night. The air was like honey. The moon

188

swam high in the sky. Reginald warmed some heather for Rosie to lie on and laid a blanket over her. He tucked his head under his tail, and with one dreaming snore was soon asleep.

In the morning Rosie was stiff but happy. 'Morning,' she called cheerily. Reginald lifted one heavy eyelid with difficulty. He was not an early riser at the best of times. 'I expect they'll be looking for me everywhere,' yawned the girl.

189

'I expect I should take you back,' said Reginald.

'Oh, not yet,' said Rosie. 'I want another ride on your back.'

And so the morning passed into afternoon, and they both enjoyed themselves so much that they forgot all about the time until Reginald decided that he wanted his afternoon snooze. Rosie, who had had enough of afternoon snoozes as a child, left Reginald in his cave and went for a walk along the brook and up the hill. She climbed

190

high above the valley. Neither she nor Reginald thought to worry about the thickening clouds above them. As she stood on the peak of the hill she suddenly felt a few drops of rainwater spatter on her cheek. 'Oh dear,' she thought, and decided to turn back. The sky was a horrible grey-green colour and the valley below was breathless and still. As Rosie turned there was a crash and a flicker of light. In an instant rain was driving into the ground like nails. Rosie was drenched.

Drops of water tumbled over her face and down her neck. Harder it fell. The rain fell so hard it hurt. It was difficult to breathe. Rosie started to run. She ran down the hill, wild and unthinking, with the water streaming over her face. Down she ran till she stumbled and fell in the mud. She lay still.

Crash! There was a crash and a flicker of light. Reginald opened his right eye.

'Are you back, Rosie? Do try to

make less noise!' Crash! The dragon sat bolt upright and knocked his head on the ceiling of his cave. Some broken rocks and dust fell on to the floor. 'Rosie?' he asked worriedly in the darkness. 'Rosie?' But there was no answer. 'Dear me,' said Reginald. 'Can she be out in this?' The dragon's saucer eyes blinked at the solid lines of grey rain outside, and its noise, like the rush of a thousand knights, assaulted his ears.

'I suppose I shall have to go and look for her.'

This was braver than it sounded, because although dragons are better protected than the strongest knight in his toughest armour, they ought not to go out in the rain as it quenches their fire. But Reginald, distressed and concerned for Rosie's safety, forgot about his own and without a moment's ado flew up into the rain. He could have flown above the rain clouds and kept dry, but then he would not have seen Rosie through the grey fleecy blanket. Instead, he let the rain ping

194

like arrows on his scales as he scanned the valley from top to bottom.

Reginald wheeled and circled, flapped and flew, till finally he saw the body of the girl lying half in water, half in mud on the side of the hill. Gently he picked her up in his mouth. Her head hung down. Her arms dangled limply. But Reginald knew she was alive because he could feel her heart beating. He knew too that her heart was like a drum, beating the end of his miserable career as a dragon.

Back in the cave he laid her carefully down, warmed her till she was dry and fed her two spoonfuls of brandy. He sat by her for hours. He sat through the night and most of the next morning, until her eyelashes quivered and her eyes opened.

'Hello,' she said weakly, 'I've been having the most wonderful dream,' and her face broke into a smile. Slowly she sat up and brushed one hand through her red hair. 'But look

196

at you!' she burst out.

Reginald felt rusty, squeaky and pathetic. His scales were dull and his snout shrivelled. Worst of all, his fire had gone out. There were no sparks left in his heart to kindle a flame. For the first time in his life he was cold and shaking.

'My fire has gone out,' he croaked. If he could have cried he possibly would have then.

Rosie touched Reginald's snout with the end of her fingers. 'You saved me,' she said, 'and you let

197

that terrible thing happen to you. Love can't always help, but sometimes it is enough,' and she breathed her warm, scented breath into the dragon's nostrils.

By some miracle Reginald's heart jumped and spluttered, and flames fanned by his own breath burned up within him. He looked on in wonder as two trickles of smoke crawled out of his nostrils. He laughed and, by mistake, singed one side of Rosie's hair. She let out a chuckle and shook her head. Reginald's fire was

198

hotter than it had ever been before. For a moment he was ecstatic and whirled round his cave with delight, then soberly he whispered, 'But the council are only going to put it out again!'

'Not if we can help it,' said Rosie, and she began to tell Reginald the plans she had dreamed when she had been asleep.

The following afternoon found Reginald sailing through the sky like a galleon, his snout pointing in the direction of Rosie's father's

199

castle. When he arrived at the castle battlements, he let out a dreadful shrieking and wailing and flew round and round the granite towers till the soldiers watching him felt sick and dizzy. Then, with remarkable dignity, Reginald descended to plant himself in the castle courtyard and roared, 'Send me the king!'

The king appeared with a chalk face, quivering.

'Miserable man! I have your daughter!'

Rosie's face appeared from under one of Reginald's wings. 'Oh, Daddy, Daddy! He can do the most dreadful things!'

'Silence!' ordered Reginald imperiously. 'Thirteen of your finest gold cups and shields, please!'

The king snapped his fingers and the soldiers stumbled over themselves in their haste to obey. The treasure was laid, glinting, in front of Reginald. The poor king was sweating hard.

'You can have your daughter

back on one condition.'

'Oh, anything!' pleaded the king.

'She must marry whom I say and whom I choose.'

The king nodded nervously.

'You will see her later. Now, go!' Reginald roared most impressively, and the king and his soldiers backed away. Reginald picked up the gold treasure in his claws and climbed into the air, shrieking all over the villages as he went.

'Do you think it worked?' he asked Rosie anxiously when they were up above the clouds.

'You were superb,' she said.

Back at the cave the two of them heaped up the new treasure on Reginald's existing meagre pile. 'Did Daddy give you this?' said Rosie. 'He never liked it. It was a present from Granny. Still – it *is* gold, I suppose. There: that looks most impressive. Now you must . . .'

'Must I?'

'Yes, it's bound to fool them.'

A little sadly, Reginald sharpened one of his claws and cut off most of

Rosie's hair. He laid it by a pile of blackened sheep bones.

'Just say she was any maiden,' suggested Rosie. 'They'll probably be so thrilled you've killed someone that they won't look too closely. Now . . . take me back – and we'll both face the music. Good luck!'

Reginald left Rosie outside her father's castle door. Of course, there had been a panic when it was found out she was missing, and then when the dragon appeared . . .

Rosie bore all the tears and

pampering well enough, only glad she had escaped from Prince Humphrey. Her father had already despatched a letter cancelling all the arrangements for her to go and see the pimply boy and he was so happy to have his daughter back that he forgot completely about marriage for a long time.

Reginald spent a couple of days blasting rocks to make the area around his cave as desolate and dragon-inhabited as possible. When Bertram finally swooped in, he was

205

obviously surprised. His copper scales rustled with disbelief.

Reginald showed him the pile of treasure, the bones and the hair, and told him that he had managed to terrify the king and a few villages.

'Well, it's a start,' said Bertram grudgingly. 'I hope you'll go on improving from now on. You've had a lucky escape.' Reginald wagged his head in agreement. Only he knew how lucky.

'I'll be back,' said Bertram. 'And

I'll put in a good word for you at the council.'

'Thanks!' shouted Reginald, but Bertram was gone.

Reginald vanished soon after that. His cave was found empty by Bertram on one of his return visits. The treasure was gone. After a few years Reginald's name was removed from the list of official dragons and his own kind forgot him.

Rosie ruled her kingdom well after her father died and married late in life. There was a legend told about her that when the moon was full she could be seen soaring through the sky on the back of a fiery dragon, but, like most legends, no one knew whether it was true or not. Rosie only winked when people asked her about it and pretended not to know what they were talking about.

The Little Mermaid

Anna Wilson

The sea king was down in the
dumps. His wife had died, and now
he was left with six tricky mer-
daughters, one bossy mer-mother-
in-law and not very much to look
forward to.

'It's always the same down here,'
he grumbled. 'Seaweed for

breakfast, seaweed for lunch and seaweed for supper, and the same old whalesong on the radio every day. Can't someone bring me some exciting news for a change?'

The littlest mer-princess swam up to her father shyly. 'I've got some news, Daddy. There's the most magnificent wreck over by the rock gardens, and a statue of a beautiful prince—'

The eldest mer-princess gave her sister a shove to shut her up and perched herself on the edge of her

211

father's throne. She flicked back her shiny hair, fluttered her eyelashes, swished her sparkling silver tail and smiled.

'*I've* got an idea, Dad.'

'What do you want, Princess?' her father grunted suspiciously. In his experience, mermaids only flicked and swished like that when they were after something.

'Why don't I go up to the kingdom over the sea and bring you back some stories?' she asked. 'Mum always told me how

212

fantastic it was up there and said she'd let me go when I got older . . . she trailed off, hoping her father would get the hint.

'Oh, all right then,' he sighed. 'Anything to break the monotony of this dark and dreary place. Off you go – no time like the present. Bring me back some excitement. And mind out for fishing nets!'

The eldest mer-princess wriggled off the rocky throne and swam off.

She swam onwards and upwards, past the old shipwreck which her little sister had mentioned.

'What does she see in that pile of junk, I wonder?' muttered the eldest mermaid, glancing at the wreck as she passed. 'And look at that statue – so ugly! It has LEGS, for cod's sake!'

Up she went, dodging a school of turtles and a family of over-excitable dolphins, on and on, weaving in and out of coral reefs and multi-coloured fish, up and up to the top of the sea. Then with a mighty PUSH she broke the surface

214

and looked around.

'I do hope no one sees me looking like this,' she grumbled, patting her hair and smoothing her scales. 'Fresh air really does nothing for my complexion.'

Luckily it was night-time, so there wasn't anyone about. In fact, there was really nothing to see but ships and stars and city lights in the distance.

'Well, I ask you! What is all the fuss about? This kingdom is even darker and drearier than our own.

No stories for Dad then.'

And with that, the mermaid plunged back down under the sea and went to find the king.

'Don't worry, Dad, it's even more boring up there than it is down here. It's all dark and quiet and nothing's happening at all. There are no fish, and the only thing to look at is a bunch of sparkly things hanging above your head. As for the people, who wants to meet anyone with LEGS anyway? Urgh!

216

Cheer up, Dad. It's much better to stick things out down here. Why don't we have a party?' she added hopefully.

'What a splendid idea!' chortled the king.

While the king and the eldest mer-princess discussed seaweed canapés and salty sea-sponge cake, the littlest mermaid slipped away to the shipwreck unnoticed.

'Why is my family so unadventurous?' she sighed. 'If only I could swim away with you,

handsome statue.' She looked
dreamily at the marble face that
was lodged in the bottom of the
wreck. She knew that all her sisters
would tease her if they found her

218

talking to a statue, but she just didn't care.

'I'll show them,' she cried. 'I'll swim away to land and seek my fortune.' She'd always been rather dramatic, even for a mer-princess.

The little mermaid swam and swam, onwards and upwards, just as her sister had done. But the sight that greeted her eyes when she reached the surface was quite different from what her sister had seen.

The sun was shining on the

219

water, making the waves sparkle
and dance, and a huge ship with
great billowing sails was making its
way towards the little mermaid.

'It's my wreck come to life!' she
cried. 'And there's my beautiful
statue, and it's alive too!'

For there, standing at the helm of the ship, was a tall, dark-haired man, whose face really did look like the statue that the little mer-princess loved so much. But this was no statue. This was Prince Gordon the Gorgeous.

'I say, chaps – look at that!' gasped Prince Gordon. 'A real, live mermaid. She's rather pretty, don't you think?' The little mermaid couldn't understand a word he said, so just stared and stared at his exquisite princely profile.

'Oh dear, he's hallucinating,' said the ship's doctor. 'Have you been eating your greens as I suggested, Your Highness? I don't want scurvy on my ship.'

'Oi, watch it, doc,' said the captain. 'It's *my* ship, not yours. And you want to stay well away from the likes of her, Your Highness. Mermaids is nothing but trouble.'

'Oh tosh, the pair of you!' laughed the prince. 'I can look after myself, whatever Mummy

222

told you. Look! She's even wearing a crown. She's a mer-princess! We're made for each other.' And he laughed again and waved at the mermaid.

The little mermaid suddenly realized that everyone on the ship was staring and pointing at her. In a fit of nerves she dived back under the waves and hid behind a rock.

'What were they all saying to him?' she cried. 'He was laughing at me – I should never have let everyone see me. Oh, I wish they

223

would all go away and leave us alone together.'

As soon as the words were out of her mouth, there was a crash of thunder, and a sharp arrow of lightning struck right over the mast of the ship. The little mermaid screamed as the ship keeled over and the sailors and Prince Gordon were hurled overboard.

'Be careful what you wish for, Fishy!' came an evil cackle. It was Meduka the sea witch, waving her tentacles in the bubbly brine and screeching insanely.

'What have you done?' shouted the little mermaid, above the roar and crash of the waves. 'You're going to kill my prince!'

'Oh, don't be so dramatic, dearie. He's all right. I've only killed the crew,' snapped the witch. 'You said you wanted him all to yourself, so why don't you go and rescue him?

225

Huh, that's gratitude for you.' And she slithered off.

The little mermaid swam as fast as her little tail would carry her to a large rock where the prince was lying limply and groaning.

'Isn't he handsome?' the little mermaid sighed, addressing her comments to Flotsam and Jetsam, a couple of seagulls who were enjoying a rough ride on the waves.

'What? Eh?' they cawed. 'Well, if you like that kind of thing, yes, I suppose so. Nice face. Shame

226

about the LEGS though.'

'Oh, go away,' the little mermaid snapped and, gathering the prince up in her arms, she swam with him back to shore. She laid him gently on the sand and kissed him, then sank back into the waves. 'Will I ever see him again?' she wondered. 'Oh, how I wish I had legs too, and not this ugly tail!'

CRASH! BASH! BANG!

'Not again . . .' cried the little mermaid, as thunder and lightning lit up the sky once more.

227

'I told you, didn't I? Be careful what you wish for, Fishy!' cackled Meduka. 'So, you want legs, eh? Well have them, then! But it'll be painful – don't say I didn't warn you.'

And with a tickle of her tentacles, Meduka turned the little mermaid's sparkling silver tail into a pair of luscious long legs.

'Much good may it do you, you silly little sea creature!' hissed the witch, slinking off into the murky depths.

'Oh! Aren't they beautiful!' gasped the little mermaid, staring in wonder at her silky new limbs. 'What did Meduka mean by "painful", I wonder? I can't feel anything at all.' The little mermaid sighed, and gazed at her handsome prince longingly. 'Wake up,' she

whispered, and kissed him again.

'Wha—?' Gorgeous Gordon awoke
with a start, a rather unattractive
trickle of drool running down his

230

cheek. 'Who are you? Why haven't you got any clothes on? And where am I?' he asked impatiently. 'I say, I was having a lovely dream about a beautiful mer-princess. At least, I think it was a dream. No, it wasn't! I remember now – she was in the water and I was on my ship . . . My ship? Where is it?' And the self-centred prince ran off, leaving the poor little mermaid to run after him. Or try to . . .

'Ow! Ouch! Now I know what Meduka meant!' screamed the

mermaid. Her legs gave way under her. The pain in her new feet was unbearable; it was like walking on broken glass. But even worse was the sound of the prince speaking, for the magic that had made the mer-princess human had also given her the gift of human speech. Now she could hear Prince Gordon wailing for his ship – and then for his mummy. 'Argh! He's a nightmare on legs!' the little mermaid shuddered. 'Who would have thought that such a handsome face could conceal such a nincompoopish nature! I wish I had a tail after all.'

And yes, one CRASH! BANG! BASH! later, Meduka the sea witch appeared in a flash of lightning.

'Save it, Grandma!' hissed the little mermaid. 'Just give me back my tail and go back to your cave.'

'All right, Miss Hoity-Toity. I suppose even I've had enough fun for one day,' agreed Meduka grudgingly, and tickled the little mermaid's feet with her tentacles once again.

ZAP! SWISH! SPLOSH!

The mer-princess was a proper mermaid once more, and truly content for the first time in her life.

'No more dreaming about marble statues for me. There's more to life than selling your tail for love, that's for sure,' she thought to

234

herself. 'For a start, there's a party to go to!'

And with that, she dived down to her father's kingdom, equipped with an adventure story that even he would find amusing.

Princess Dragonbreath

Fiona Dunbar

The king and queen of Flamovia
were desperate for a child and heir
to the throne. But many years
passed and no child came until at
last, long after they had abandoned
all hope, a daughter was born.
Sadly, the queen died in childbirth,

but her baby girl was very much alive and brimming with health. Despite his grief for the queen, the king of Flamovia was overjoyed.

'This precious child shall want for nothing!' he proudly proclaimed. After a decent interval, he arranged for a lavish christening party and named his daughter

Magnificentia Joyous Heavenly-Gift Divine – Maggie for short. He enlisted no fewer than twelve fairy godmothers to ensure her welfare.

The day of the christening arrived and people gathered at the palace from all four corners of the kingdom of Flamovia, to cheer the guests as they arrived. The palace filled up with courtiers, resplendent in their finery. Outside the gates, the poorest citizens crowded around to glimpse what they could of the ceremony inside the palace.

238

After the christening, the guests enjoyed a lavish banquet. Then the king summoned the twelve fairy godmothers. The first one waved her wand about Princess Maggie's head and said, 'She shall have silken locks the colour of fire!'

Then the second fairy godmother came forward. 'She'll have boundless energy and never tire!' she said, because it rhymed with what fairy godmother number one had just said, and if there's one thing fairy godmothers *love*, it's rhyming

239

couplets. In fact, they are unable to speak any other way.

And so it continued, with successive fairy godmothers bestowing ever more impressive gifts on the infant princess. Every time another one came forth and pronounced that Princess Maggie would have a beautiful singing voice, or skin like alabaster, there would be gasps of delight. What a splendid young woman she would grow up to be! How lovely and talented in every way! How she would be admired and adored by all who met her!

Finally, it was the turn of fairy godmother number twelve, whose name was Justina. She stepped forward and gazed around the room at all the fawning, simpering faces of the nobility, with their powdered wigs and their jewels and frills. Then she thought of all the poor people she had passed on the way to the palace, with their filthy ragged clothes, lopsided faces and withered legs. 'Why should one

child be so unfairly favoured?'
thought Justina. 'It's beginning to
make me feel quite sick!' Her plan
had been to bestow a fine artistic
talent on the princess, but now she
had completely gone off the idea.
All the same, she knew she would
have to say something. The king
and all his courtiers beamed at her
expectantly. She stepped forward.
She did a little twirl ending with a
flourish of her wand and a curtsy.

The king sighed. 'Ahem. May we
know what gift you have for my

242

little Magnificentia?'

What could Justina say? That the princess would have a lop-sided face, or a withered leg? No, she couldn't; that would be far too cruel. Then, at last, she hit on an idea. She batted her eyelashes and fluttered her wings. 'The princess shall have her every wish,' declared Justina. 'None must be denied her!'

There were 'oohs' and 'aahs' all around. What a lucky princess!

The king, however, merely shrugged. 'Well, that goes without

243

saying,' he said. 'I have already decreed it myself.'

'Forgive me, Your Majesty, my splendourous master,' Justina added quickly, 'but any wish denied will result in *disaster*!'

The king nodded, smiling. 'Excellent!' he pronounced. 'It's comforting to know that my darling Magnificentia Joyous Heavenly-Gift Divine will be protected from any distress in this way. Thank you, Justina.'

But he didn't spot the glint in

Justina's eye as she turned away. It was a look that said, *Just you wait* . . .

From that day forth, the entire royal household was terrified of ever saying 'no' to Princess Maggie. The years passed and the young princess had her way about absolutely everything. For her birthdays, she would think up outlandish presents, and every year her requests became grander and more extreme. For her sixth birthday she got seven ponies, one for each day of the week, each a different colour of the rainbow.

For her seventh birthday, Princess Maggie wanted all the chocolate in the whole of the kingdom of Flamovia. The princess was granted her wish.

You will not be surprised to learn that, by now, Princess Maggie was the most spoiled child you could possibly meet. She was heartless, rude and dreadfully selfish.

Nevertheless, the king doted on her. One week before Princess Maggie's eighth birthday, he went to her chamber and asked his

246

daughter what she wanted.

The princess, lounging on her golden bed stuffed with swans' feathers, looked up from her storybook. 'A weal live pet dwagon!' she announced breathlessly. 'There's a lovely picture of one in my book, I would so love to have one, darling Pops!'

'Ah,' said the king. This was worrying; the last ever live dragon had been slain two years before. 'Might be a bit of a problem there, my precious one.'

Princess Maggie put her book down and stared wide-eyed at him. '*What* did you say, Popsie?'

'Oh nothing, it's just, er . . .'

'You don't mean to tell me I *can't* have a dwagon, do you, Daddy?' Princess Maggie gazed at him in disbelief. The prospect of not getting something she wanted gave her such an unfamiliar feeling she began to turn a delicate shade of green. 'Oh my!' she cried. 'I think I'm going to be sick!'

The king began to panic. Not

248

only was he worried about the effect this news was having on his little darling, he was also only too aware that she simply *must* have her wish or disaster would befall them. But there was no getting away from the fact that there were no dragons. He was stuck.

'Of course you may have a dragon, dearest,' he said at last. He would worry later about where he would find one.

And so the day arrived: Princess Maggie's eighth birthday. It was a very grand occasion, and after a splendid feast the princess would open all her hundreds of presents from well-wishers. The princess whirred through these, bits of paper flying everywhere. Then, tossing the last one aside, she demanded, 'OK, where's my dwagon?'

The king beamed at her, concealing his anxiety as best he could. He gave the signal, and the doors of the banqueting hall opened to the sound of trumpets blasting. In wheeled a large, specially designed

250

open carriage festooned with ribbons.
Inside was a greenish brown, scaly
creature with a long snout and very,
very short legs, about the size and
shape of a crocodile. Because it *was*
a crocodile. It was a very sleepy
crocodile, because it had been
sedated so that it didn't decide to
take a big bite out of the princess.
Attached to it, as convincingly as
possible, were two scaly, greenish-
brownish fake wings. The carriage
was wheeled up to Princess Maggie,
who clapped her hands with glee.

251

'Ooh goody goody, my vewy own dwagon!' she squealed. 'Take it out, let me have a pwoper look.'

And so the 'dragon' was unveiled and brought to the princess's feet, attached to a golden leash. Princess Maggie stared at it.

'Why's it so small?' she asked. 'I thought dwagons were much bigger than that.'

'Well, my little rosebud,' said the king. 'He is only a young dragon.'

'Is that why he's got such short legs as well?' asked the princess.

'Er, yes, that's right,' said the king.

'He doesn't seem like a *pwoper* dwagon to me at all,' insisted Princess Maggie, disappointed.

'I think I will have to put him to the test.'

'What test would that be, my precious?' said the king, sweat beading his brow.

'It's easy, Popsie. If he's a pwoper dwagon, he'll be able to bweathe fire.' The princess slipped off her seat, took hold of the golden leash and led the crocodile over to a gigantic fireplace. 'OK, stupid dwagon,' she ordered, 'do your stuff!'

The winged crocodile just stood

there, eyes drooping.

'Well, come on!' shrieked the princess.

'Darling Maggie, he probably doesn't feel like it right now,' said the king gently.

Princess Maggie wasn't listening. 'Come on, stupid dwagon, like this—' and she opened her mouth wide and went 'HURRR!' into the fireplace.

'Sweetheart—' said the king.

'*HURRR!*' went the princess, then put her hands on her hips and waited for the 'dragon' to do the same.

The crocodile merely swayed a little, then rested its head on the floor and fell asleep. Furious, Princess Maggie marched up to him, grabbed him by his fake wings and shook him.

'No, don't do that!' cried the king. 'You'll—'

At that moment, the fake wings came off in Princess Maggie's hands. 'AAH!' she gasped in horror. 'You lied to me!' she yelled. 'This is

256

no dwagon, it's only a stupid *cwocodile*! How dare you give me such a wubbish pwesent, Daddy!' she went on, stamping her foot petulantly. 'I insist I get a weal dwagon this vewy instant!'

And now, eight years too late, the King finally realized what a monster he had allowed his daughter to become. 'No, you cannot have one,' he retorted angrily, 'because there *aren't* any dragons!'

Gasps of consternation echoed

257

around the hall. Nobody had *ever* said the word 'no' to Princess Magnificentia. And what is more, everyone knew of Fairy Godmother Justina's prediction; they knew that this could only spell disaster for the royal family. Everyone held their breath as they waited to see what would happen.

Princess Maggie gawped at the king. Her brow furrowed, her eyes filled with tears. And then, she let out an enormous, deafening . . .

BURP!

258

Those seated nearest to the princess felt the blast of this noxious wind, and it blew them sideways. 'Eurgh!' they exclaimed, unable to hide their disgust. For Princess Magnificentia's burp smelled very strongly of extremely hot curry. The fiery chilli-pepper gases brought tears to their eyes. They covered their faces with handkerchiefs and coughed profusely.

'What's going on?' cried the king. Then Princess Maggie turned to her father and burped again. It hit him in the face like a ball of fire. 'Oh good heavens!' cried the king, and he summoned the royal physician immediately.

The royal physician examined the princess carefully, during which she burped seven times. Every burp was as fiery and stinky as the last. Then the doctor turned to the king, eyes streaming, and said, 'I'm very sorry, Your Majesty – *cough, cough* – but it appears – *cough!* – that this has come about as a result of the fairy godmother's prediction at the

princess's christening. Therefore –
cough! – I can do nothing to help.'

'Owoowoowoo!' howled the
princess, distressed at this news, then
burped again.

The king was utterly distraught.
He summoned the royal solicitor,
who specialized in fairy-godmother-
spells-and-predictions law. 'How
long will this go on for?' he asked.
The royal solicitor consulted his
files. 'I'm very sorry, Your Majesty,'
he replied. 'But it says here that all
predictions made by fairy

261

godmothers at christenings will last until such time as the subject – Princess Magnificentia in this case – receives love's first kiss.'

BURP! went the princess. Another ball of fiery gas hurtled across the room.

The king put his head in his hands. 'Oh but this is terrible! How will my precious Maggie ever receive love's first kiss with such foul reeking eruptions issuing forth every few minutes? She was supposed to fall in love with a handsome prince

and live happily ever after, but now
. . . no handsome prince will ever
want to come near her. My poor
child is doomed!'

'Owoowoowoo!' howled the
princess.

And so it was that Princess Maggie
became known as 'Princess
Dragonbreath' – though never to
her face, of course – or in front of
the devastated king. For ten more
years she continued with her fiery
burps, during which time she grew

into a young woman. She might have been truly lovely, with her flame-red hair, alabaster skin and so on; charming, too, with all the talents bestowed on her by her fairy godmothers. However, because of the awful burps – and the cruel nickname, which she soon found out about – she preferred not to meet people and barely spoke to anyone. Instead, she shut herself away and filled the empty hours eating chocolate cake, not caring that it was making her fat. Why

264

should she? The chilli-pepper belches
kept everyone away, so it didn't
seem to matter what she looked
like. She had no friends and no

prospect of a princely boyfriend or a husband.

Then, one day, there was a knock at princess Dragonbreath's bedroom door. 'Go away!' snapped the princess, and then she said, '*Uuurp!*'

'Excuse me, Princess,' came a man's voice from behind the door. 'I've come to sweep your chimney.'

'It doesn't need sweeping,' insisted Princess Dragonbreath. 'Now go away, *uuurrp!*'

But the young man strode right

in. 'Good afternoon,' he said, nodding politely. He went over to the fireplace, carrying his chimney sweep's brush. He was black with soot from head to foot.

Princess Dragonbreath was so taken aback she said nothing. Not just because he was so forthright, but because he didn't reel in disgust at the eye-wateringly putrid smell that filled the room. In fact he didn't seem to notice it at all. She sat and watched as he carefully laid out dustsheets, then set about his

work. During this time, the princess
burped seventeen times, but the
chimney sweep didn't bat an eyelid.
'I think I'm in love,' thought
Princess Dragonbreath, and while
the young man was up the chimney
she went over to her dressing table
and fixed herself up a bit. She took
her nightcap off and brushed her
silky, flame-red locks. She rouged
her cheeks and put on her prettiest
shimmery shawl.

Presently the chimney sweep
emerged, even blacker than before,

and began to roll up his dustsheet.

'Ahem,' said Princess Dragonbreath, and the young man glanced up. She noticed he had ice-blue eyes. 'Would you – *uuurp!* – care for a slice of chocolate cake?' she added.

Still the chimney sweep did not shy away from the force of her terrible burps, nor did tears come to his eyes, nor any sign of disgust show itself on his face. In fact he was staring right at her. He just smiled and thought, 'I didn't notice before, but she's a fine-looking young woman, if a bit on the plump side.'

'Well yes, thank you, Your Highness,' he said, 'don't mind if I do.'

So the two of them sat and munched on chocolate cake, the princess regularly burping her hot-curry burps. The sweep just nodded and smiled. 'It's very tasty,' he said.

The princess wanted to say something to this fascinating young man, but, every time she tried, she lost her nerve and either burped or dived into another slice of cake.

The chimney sweep, too, found himself quite entranced. But he didn't dare say a word, as he had no idea what one was supposed to say to a princess. So eventually he said, 'Well, must be going,' and got up to leave.

'Oh no, don't go!' cried Princess Dragonbreath, clutching his soot-covered arm and sending a black cloud on to her pink silk rug.

271

The chimney sweep blinked at her.

'That is ... I ... Why don't you mind my burps?' said the princess at last.

'Should I?' he asked.

'Well, you're the first person I've ever met who didn't cough and cwy at the fire in my bweath.'

'Fire?' said the chimney sweep.

'Yes, you know. Foul hot spicy blast. You don't mean to say you haven't – *uurp!* – noticed?'

'Oh no, I wouldn't notice that,'

272

said the young man. 'I come from a long line of dragon-slayers. We're immune to fiery breath – it's in our blood.'

'Did you say "dwagon-slayers"?' asked Princess Maggie, astounded.

'Well, yes . . . sort of,' said the chimney sweep. 'Dragons have really bad breath, you know, even when they're not puffing flames. It's all the brimstone they eat. Only there's no need for dragon-slaying any more, since I killed the last one twelve years ago. I was only sixteen, yet already I had slain seven dragons; I was the best dragon-slayer ever! But I did such a good job of it, I put myself out of work. So ever since then I've had to eke out a living sweeping chimneys.'

The princess was reminded of that fateful birthday ten years before, when she had been so intent on having her pet dragon that she had been utterly horrid to her poor old Pops. 'How ghastly I was!' she thought. And something else was bothering her too. 'But what about the noise?' she asked. 'Of the – *uurp!* – that.'

'Noise?' said the chimney sweep. 'I wouldn't notice any noise. I'm as deaf as a post. All the roaring of those dragons did permanent damage to my tender young ears, and I've been deaf ever since.'

'But you can hear me – *uurp!* – talk!' exclaimed the princess.

'No I can't,' explained the chimney sweep. 'I lip-read.'

'That explains why you didn't go away when I told you to!'

275

exclaimed the princess. 'You couldn't – *uurp!* – lip-wead fwom behind the door. Oh, Mister – *what* did you say your name was?'

'I didn't,' said the chimney sweep. 'It's James Gallant Steed-Rider, but you can call me Jim.'

'Oh, Jim!' cried Princess Dragonbreath. 'It's fate – we were destined to meet!' So saying, she pulled him towards her and gave him the biggest, chocolatiest – *smelliest* – smackeroony.

And Jim, completely untroubled

276

by her reeking breath, kissed
Princess Dragonbreath back.

From that moment forth,
Princess Dragonbreath once more
became Princess Maggie, and she
never belched again for the rest of

277

her life. Not even the daintiest odour-free burplet passed her lips. She was so overjoyed, she no longer needed to fill her every waking hour with chocolate cake, and very soon was back to her normal slender shape. Everyone was astounded at her beauty. Ten years of such dreadful humiliation had also changed Princess Maggie's personality completely; she was no longer self-centred and rude. She was kind to her father, and instantly made friends with everyone from the grandest duchess to the lowliest maid.

The chimney sweep, Jim, turned out to be quite astonishingly handsome, once he'd been bathed and groomed. The king was so grateful to him for rescuing his darling daughter from a lifetime of stinky breath he didn't care a jot that Jim wasn't a prince, or that he had no money, and awarded him a knighthood. Thus, Jim, the ex-dragon-slayer, at last became *Sir* James Gallant Steed-Rider.

And now, eighteen years after the big christening party, came another great celebration in the kingdom of Flamovia: the wedding of Princess Magnificentia Joyous Heavenly-Gift Divine and her gallant Sir Jim. And yes, they did live happily – and burplessly – ever after.

Although they didn't half fart whenever they had beans for dinner.

Acknowledgements

The compiler and publishers wish to thank the following for permission to use copyright material:

Fiona Dunbar 'Princess Dragonbreath', by permission of The Agency (London) Ltd © Fiona Dunbar 2005. All rights reserved and enquiries to The Agency (London) Ltd, 24 Pottery Lane, London Wl 1 4LZ, fax: 0207 727 9037; **Alan Durant** 'The Frog Princess', by permission of The Agency (London) Ltd © Alan Durant 2005. All rights reserved and enquiries to The Agency (London) Ltd, 24 Pottery Lane, London W11 4LZ, fax: 0207 727 9037; **Sally Gardner** 'The Princess and the Pea' from *A Book of Princesses – Five Favourite Princess Stories,* by permission of Orion Children's Books, a division of the Orion Publishing Group Ltd, Orion House, 5 Upper St Martin's Lane, London WC2H 9EA, © Sally Gardner 1997; **Tony Mitton** 'Cinderella Rap' from *Royal Raps* by Tony Mitton, by permission of Orchard Books © Tony Mitton 1996 First published by Orchard Books (1996), a division of The Watts Publishing Group Limited, 96 Leonard Street, London EC2A 4XD; **Saviour Pirotta** 'The Twelve Dancing Princesses' from *The Sleeping Princess and other Fairy Stories,* by permission of Orchard Books. © Saviour Pirotta 2002. First published by Orchard Books (2002), a division of The Watts Publishing Group Limited, 96 Leonard Street, London EC2A 4XD; **William Raeper** 'The Reluctant Dragon and the Wilful Princess', from *The Troll and the Butterfly* by William Raeper, by kind permission of the Estate of William Raeper c/o Rogers, Coleridge & White Ltd, 20 Powis Mews, London W11 1JN, © William Raeper 1987 First published by Andre Deutsch; **Barbara Sleigh** 'A Wreath of Wild Roses', by permission of The Agency (London) Ltd © Barbara Sleigh 1979. First published by Hodder & Stoughton Children's Books. All rights reserved and enquiries to The Agency (London) Ltd, 24 Pottery Lane, London W11 4LZ, fax: 0207 727 9037; **Jeremy Strong** 'The Sixteenth Princess', from *The Karate Princess,* by permission of David Higham Associates Ltd on behalf of the author © Jeremy Strong 1989; **Anna Wilson** 'The Princess's New Nose', by permission of The Agency (London) Ltd © Anna Wilson 2005. All rights reserved and enquiries to The Agency (London) Ltd, 24 Pottery Lane, London W11 4LZ, fax: 0207 727 9037; **Anna Wilson** 'The Little Mermaid', by permission of The Agency (London) Ltd © Anna Wilson 2005. All rights reserved and enquiries to The Agency (London) Ltd, 24 Pottery Lane, London W11 4LZ, fax: 0207 727 9037.

A selected list of titles available from Macmillan Children's Books

The prices shown below are correct at the time of going to press. However, Macmillan Publishers reserves the right to show new retail prices on covers which may differ from those previously advertised.

Gwyneth Rees

Fairy Treasure	0 330 43730 5	£4.99
Cosmo and the Magic Sneeze	0 330 43729 1	£4.99

Julie Bertagna

The Ice-Cream Machine	0 330 43746 1	£3.99
The Ice-Cream Machine 2	0 330 43403 9	£3.99

All Pan Macmillan titles can be ordered from our website, www.panmacmillan.com, or from your local bookshop and are also available by post from:

Bookpost, PO Box 29, Douglas, Isle of Man IM99 1BQ
Credit cards accepted. For details:
Telephone: 01624 836000
Fax: 01624 670923
Email: bookshop@enterprise.net
www.bookpost.co.uk

Free postage and packing in the United Kingdom